THE STORY OF
CHOPSTICKS

BY

Ying Chang Compestine

ILLUSTRATED BY

YongSheng Xuan

Holiday House / New York

LONG AGO all Chinese people ate with their hands, including members of a family named Kang.

The Kang family had three boys: Pan, Ting, and Kùai. All the boys loved to eat, especially the youngest, Kùai. Yet Kùai never seemed to get enough food. He was always hungry.

One afternoon Mama Kang called out. "It's time to get ready for dinner. Papa, cut the chicken. Pan, peel the sweet potatoes. Ting, start the fire, and Kùai, get water from the well."

Wonderful smells soon filled the house. Kùai's tummy rumbled. If only I could eat my food right away, he thought. But if I pick it up too soon, it burns my fingers. And if I wait too long, my brothers get most of it and leave me nothing. He thought and thought.

"Time for dinner! Everybody wash hands!" shouted Mama.

They all ran to the well. Pan brought the bucket. Ting lowered it. Papa hauled it up. Kùai waited.

"I'm going to be first," he said.

"You don't have to rush," said Mama. "The food is still too hot to eat."

Kùai said nothing, but his lips held a smile. As he washed, he splashed water all over.

"Kùai!" scolded Papa. "Look at the mess you made. The bucket is nearly empty. Ting, help me refill it."

While they got more water, Kùai ran back to the house.

Kùai plucked two long twigs from the kindling by the stove and speared a chicken leg with one stick and a big chunk of sweet potato with the other. Then he started to eat. The food was still hot, yet he didn't burn his fingers. Best of all, he didn't have to race his older brothers. For once he was going to get enough to eat.

When his family finally returned from the well, they were surprised. Ting understood immediately. He ran to the kindling and got himself two long twigs. Pan and Papa were right behind him. In a moment they were climbing over each other, wrestling for twigs. "Ai yo!" they cried.

Kùai never stopped eating. After a while things settled down. Everyone had a pair of twigs, even Mama.

"We should give these sticks a name," suggested Pan.

"Let's call them 'Kùai zi' to honor Kùai, the 'quick one' in our family," said Ting. Kùai smiled at his brother.

This was the first time that a family in China ate dinner with sticks instead of their hands.

A few days later Mama came home very excited. "Mr. Wang is holding a wedding for his daughter. It will be a big banquet. Everyone is invited."

On the day of the wedding Papa carried a bundle of red silk, a symbol of celebration. Mama carried a basket of fruit and nuts, a symbol of their wish that the new couple would soon have many children.

Unknown to anyone else, the boys brought something, too.

When they arrived, Kùai led his brothers to join the other children. "Look at that food! I never saw a table as big as this one."

Ting grinned. "See the steam rising from that fish. It smells so good! It will be a long time before anyone can pick it up."

Pan whispered to his brothers. "See those girls rolling up their sleeves? They don't want their clothes to get dirty."

The children stared at the food like starved wolves. Servants carried out more meat and vegetable dishes. Dumplings, egg rolls, and rice cakes soon followed. All the children moved in closer, getting ready to strike.

Kùai looked at his brothers. "Let's go!" The Kang boys whipped out their sticks and attacked the Butterfly chicken, Wealthy Peony beef, steamed buns, rice cakes, and especially the Sweet Eight Treasures Rice Pudding.

The other children stared at them. Some tried to grab food for themselves. "Ai yo!" they yelped. "It's too hot."

The smart ones ran off to find their own sticks. Before long all the children were searching for sticks. Some even climbed trees to break off the branches.

"What is all this noise?" asked Mr. Wang. Soon all the grown-ups were gathered around the banquet table, even the bride and groom.

Children held all kinds of sticks. A tall boy held two large branches. A toddler carried tiny twigs. Some children had their arms full.

Papa opened his mouth to scold the boys. When he did, Kùai put a big piece of meat in his mouth. "Try the chicken!" he cried. Now Papa was too busy chewing to yell at them.

But Mama wasn't too busy. "Boys!" she cried. "Boys—" Pan put a big piece of rice cake in her mouth. Now Mama couldn't scold either.

Mr. Wang looked sternly at the running children. He glowered at Mama and Papa, who were chewing away. "AI YO!" he cried.

A hush fell over the crowd. Mr. Wang turned red. He began to shake. He was laughing! Everyone else started to laugh, too.

Mr. Lee, the village wise man, stepped forward. He looked very serious. After he raised his hand for attention, the crowd fell silent.

Mr. Lee pointed at the children's sticks. "Whose idea was this?" he thundered.

The Kang boys looked at one another. Pan stepped forward. "It was my idea. Please don't blame my brother."

Then Ting bowed carefully to Mr. Lee. "It was my idea. Please don't blame my brother."

Papa walked over to Mr. Lee. "It is my fault, Mr. Lee, we did not teach our children manners. Please—"

Mr. Lee gestured for silence. "I must meet with the village leaders tomorrow morning. Your whole family shall attend."

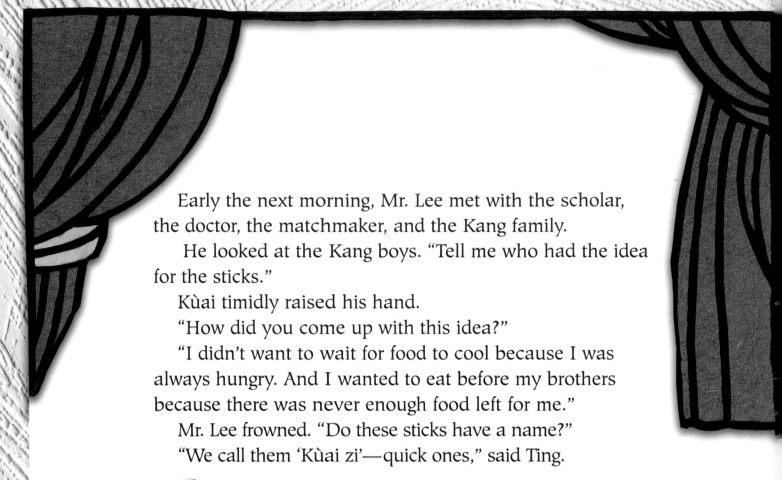

Early the next morning, Mr. Lee met with the scholar, the doctor, the matchmaker, and the Kang family.

He looked at the Kang boys. "Tell me who had the idea for the sticks."

Kùai timidly raised his hand.

"How did you come up with this idea?"

"I didn't want to wait for food to cool because I was always hungry. And I wanted to eat before my brothers because there was never enough food left for me."

Mr. Lee frowned. "Do these sticks have a name?"

"We call them 'Kùai zi'—quick ones," said Ting.

Mr. Lee turned to the other elders. "I would like your suggestions for the proper way to eat."

The doctor said, "We should let our elders begin the meal."

"We should not stir food in serving bowls," said the matchmaker.

"The food should be cut into small pieces so that it's easy to eat," said the scholar. Then he added, "What should we do about these Kùai zi?"

Mr. Lee smoothed his long white beard and took a sip of tea. "None of these rules conflicts with using Kùai zi to eat. After much thought, I say that eating with Kùai zi is a good idea. I will write a report and send it to the emperor."

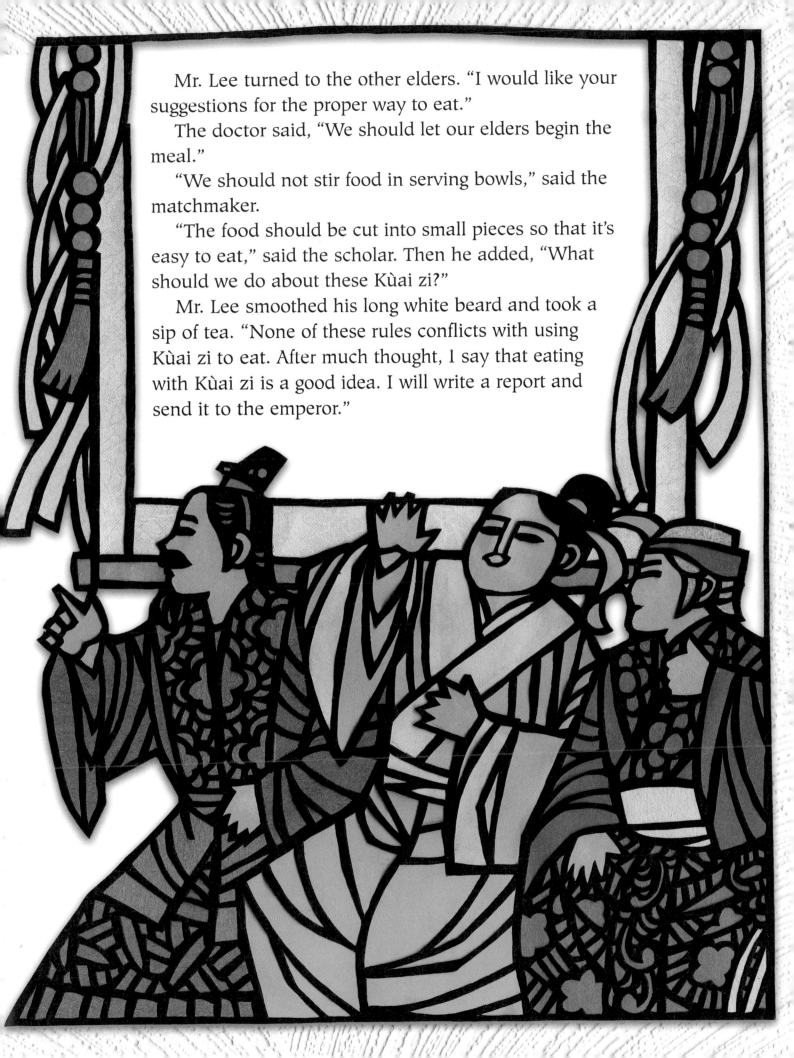

The emperor also liked eating with Kùai zi. Before long people were using them in every part of China. From there Kùai zi spread to other countries, including America. There they are called chopsticks, "quick sticks."

As for the Kang family, they opened the very first
chopstick factory. Their chopsticks, beautifully decorated
with dragons, phoenixes, flowers, and lucky letters,
became famous.

Kùai was the happiest boy in China. His food was never
too cold, and he always got enough to eat . . .

. . . sometimes even too much!

AUTHOR'S NOTE

Chopsticks originated in China, perhaps as early as the eleventh century B.C.E. They are called "Kùai zi" (pronounced *KHWY-zzuh*) in Mandarin Chinese, which translates to "quick ones." In the pidgin English used by Chinese and European traders of old, "chop" meant "quick." Hence "quick sticks" became "chopsticks." Chopsticks are commonly made of unadorned wood, bamboo, and plastic. Some are intricately crafted from ivory, porcelain, or silver.

Confucianism, one of the dominant philosophies in China, placed strong emphasis on good manners. The Chinese were taught that it was bad manners to have a guest struggle cutting up food. Instead the host should prepare the food in the kitchen. By substituting chopsticks for knives, the Chinese showed their respect for the scholar over the warrior.

Over the centuries the Chinese have developed several rules for eating with chopsticks.

✦ The meal should not start until the eldest person at the table raises his chopsticks.
✦ Chopsticks should not stand upright in a bowl of rice. This looks too much like a tombstone on a grave.
✦ Chopsticks should not be set lengthwise across the rice bowl. This is considered symbolic of a coffin. Instead, they should be placed on a chopstick stand to the right of the bowl, resting the tips on the stand.
✦ Chopsticks should not be rattled against the bowl It's believed this will break the wealth of future generations.

To my own Kùai, Vinson Ming-Da, with much love!—Y. C. C.

In loving memory of Ya Wu and Jesse Lei—Y. X.

How to use chopsticks

1. Place one chopstick in the hollow between your thumb and index finger. Then rest the lower part of the stick on the tip of your ring finger.

2. Insert the second stick above the first one. Hold it the way you would hold a pencil.

3. Bring the tips of the two sticks together by moving the second stick with your index and middle fingers. The first chopstick should remain still.

Beginners can band the sticks together at the top and hold them close to the bottom.

Now you can use chopsticks to pick up food!

Sweet Eight Treasures Rice Pudding

MAKES 4 SERVINGS
PREPARATION TIME: 10 MINUTES
1 1/2 cups cooked warm sweet rice
1/2 cup chopped fresh mango
1/4 cup raisins
1/4 cup green candied cherries
1/4 cup dried tart cherries
1/4 cup chopped candied pineapple
1/2 cup almond butter
1/4 cup maple syrup

1. Line the bottom of a 6-or 8-inch bowl with plastic wrap. **2.** Decorate the bottom of the bowl with the mango and other fruit. **3.** Pack half of the rice in the bowl in an even layer. **4.** Spread the almond butter and syrup over the rice. **5.** Cover with remaining rice. Flatten firmly. **6.** Invert onto a platter and serve warm.

Text copyright © 2001 by Ying Chang Compestine
Illustrations copyright © 2001 by YongSheng Xuan
All Rights Reserved
The illustrations were created with cut paper in traditional Chinese style.
Printed in the United States of America   www.holidayhouse.com   First Edition
Library of Congress Cataloging-in-Publication Data
Compestine, Ying Chang.
The story of chopsticks / by Ying Chang Compestine; illustrated by YongSheng Xuan.—1st ed.
p. cm.   Summary: When Kùai cannot get enough to eat, he begins using sticks
to grab food too hot for the hands, and soon all of China uses Kùai zi, or chopsticks.
ISBN 0-8234-1526-0 (hardcover)   [1. Chopsticks—Fiction. 2. China—Fiction.]
I. Xuan, YongSheng, ill. II. Title.   PZ7.C73615 St 2001   [E]–dc21   00-039615